# MERRY CHRISTMAS, OLD ARMADILLO

LARRY DANE BRIMNER

# MERRY CHRISTMAS, OLD ARMADILLO

ILLUSTRATED BY
DOMINIC CATALANO

BOYDS MILLS PRESS

For mi hijo, and for Kent Brown and Jody Taylor, who know the charm of armadillos
—L. D. B.

For Mary, my inspiration, my best friend, *and* the love of my life!
—D. C.

Text copyright © 1995 by Larry Dane Brimner
Illustrations copyright © 1995 by Dominic Catalano
All rights reserved

Published by Caroline House
Boyds Mills Press, Inc.
A Highlights Company
815 Church Street
Honesdale, Pennsylvania 18431
Printed in Mexico

Publisher Cataloging-in-Publication Data
Brimner, Larry Dane.
   Merry Christmas, Old Armadillo / by Larry Dane Brimner ;
illustrated by Dominic Catalano.—1st ed.
(32)p. : col. ill. ;    cm.
Summary : Thinking his friends have forgotten him at Christmas,
Old Armadillo goes to sleep, but he awakens to find that his
friends have decorated his house and a tree for the holiday.
ISBN 1-56397-354-5
1. Friendship—Fiction—Juvenile literature. 2. Christmas stories—
Juvenile fiction. (1. Friendship—Fiction. 2. Christmas stories.)
I. Catalano, Dominic, ill. II. Title.
   (E)    1995    CIP    AC
Library of Congress Catalog Card Number 94-79155

First edition, 1995
Book designed by Tim Gillner
The text of this book is set in 15-point Zapf Calligraphy.
The illustrations are done in pastels.
Distributed by St. Martin´s Press

10 9 8 7 6 5 4 3

**O**ld Armadillo lived all alone in a *casita* on a mesa above the tiny village of Santa Rosa.

One Christmas Eve, bells rang out from the village church and choir voices sailed on air. At the sounds, Old Armadillo perked up and went to the door. "Merry Christmas!" he called, swinging it wide. But nobody was there.

At his gate, Old Armadillo looked this way and that. He looked that way and this. But there was only the sound of the church bells and the choir voices and the gentle *shhhhh shhhhh* of the *ristra* as it swayed against the gate in the breeze.

Sighing, Old Armadillo brushed away a tear and checked his letter basket one more time. It was still empty. He thought: Christmas! What's all the fuss! And, glum and brooding, he shuffled back inside, sat down by the fire, and drifted off to sleep—kicking up a snore that rattled the windows.

*Outside . . .*

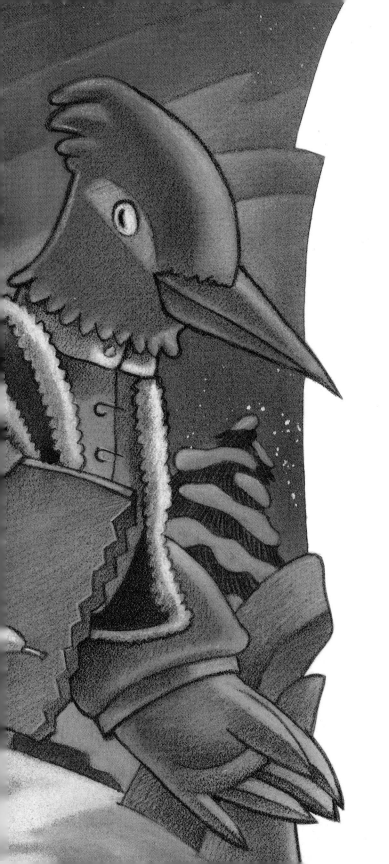

Someone tiptoed here and there in the garden. It was Roadrunner, and he was setting out the *luminarias*. They glimmered everywhere. Even the branches of the giant saguaro outside Old Armadillo's casita glowed softly against the night sky.

Inside . . . Old Armadillo kept on snoring.

*Outside . . .*

Peccary was puffing from her climb. "I hope I'm not late," she said.

Roadrunner shook his head and helped Peccary hang her piney wreath on the ancient door.

Inside . . . Old Armadillo kept on snoring.

*Outside . . .*

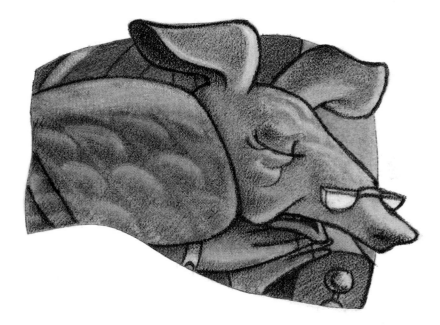

Voices whispered. "I hope these will do." Coyote set down a crate of apples and grapefruits and pears. In the light of the luminarias, they shimmered red and yellow and green.

Roadrunner nodded. "They're perfect," he said.

Inside . . . Old Armadillo kept on snoring.

*Outside . . .*

Voices oohed and aahed. Tortoise had brought a cactus with beautiful red blossoms. Raccoon offered a water lily.

Inside . . . Old Armadillo kept on snoring.

*Outside . . .*

Feet paced, and eyes peered down the path into the darkness. "Oh—where is Bear?" asked Roadrunner.

"AAAH!"

"That sounds like him now," Peccary said.

"AAAH!" Bear yawned again and patted his mouth with his paw. "I'm late, I know. I can sleep through almost anything. But—but not this."

"Did you bring it?" asked Roadrunner. "You didn't forget, did you?"

"I'm sleepy," Bear said, sounding hurt, "not forgetful."

"Let's do it, then," Roadrunner said.

Inside . . . Old Armadillo kept on snoring.

*Outside . . .* paws tried the knocker.

Inside . . . Old Armadillo kept on snoring.

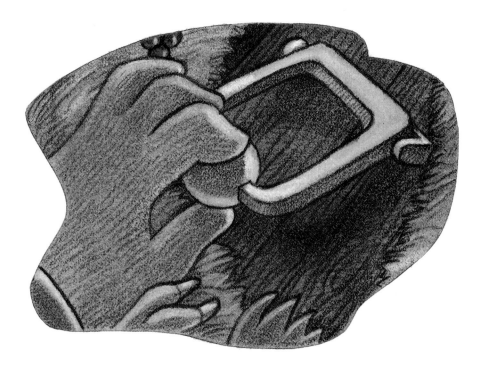

*Outside . . .* noses pressed against
windowpanes and knuckles rapped on the glass.

Inside . . . Old Armadillo kept on snoring.

*Outside . . .*

Fists hammered the door and voices shouted.

Inside . . . Old Armadillo kept on snoring.

*Outside . . .*

It got quiet and still.

Inside . . . it suddenly became just as quiet and still, and Old Armadillo woke with a jump. "Who's there?" he called.
"It's us! It's just us!"

 **O**ld Armadillo went to the door. He thought:
Such a bother! Such a fuss!
     And out he went.

The night air had become crisp, and stars now sparkled white in the deep-blue sky. "Merry Christmas!" voices chimed.

"My old friends!" Old Armadillo said, surprised. "It has been a long time. I thought you had forgotten me."

"It *has* been a long time," said Roadrunner. "But a friend is not easily forgotten."

Old Armadillo looked into the garden beyond his friends, and the Christmas tree nearly took his breath away. "Ooooh!" he said.

"Merry Christmas, Old Armadillo," said his friends. Then one by one their voices joined with those of the choir in the church far below. And when the festive bells began to ring out again, Old Armadillo thought: Christmas! Such a wonderful fuss!

*"Merry Christmas, everyone!"*

And that Christmas Eve, on a mesa above Santa Rosa, the joyous sound of friendship and love filled the night.